For Will,
with love – CH

For Jen
and Gabs – MM

WHO WILL SING MY PUFF-A-BYE?
A BODLEY HEAD BOOK 0 370 32666 0

First published in Great Britain
in 2004 by The Bodley Head,
an imprint of Random House Children's Books

1 3 5 7 9 10 8 6 4 2

Set in Bookman Old Style

RANDOM HOUSE CHILDREN'S BOOKS
61–63 Uxbridge Road, London W5 5SA
A division of The Random House Group Ltd

RANDOM HOUSE AUSTRALIA (PTY) LTD
20 Alfred Street, Milsons Point, Sydney,
New South Wales 2061, Australia

RANDOM HOUSE NEW ZEALAND LTD
18 Poland Road, Glenfield, Auckland 10, New Zealand

RANDOM HOUSE (PTY) LTD
Endulini, 5A Jubilee Road, Parktown 2193, South Africa

THE RANDOM HOUSE GROUP Limited Reg. No. 954009
www.kidsatrandomhouse.co.uk

A CIP catalogue record for this book is available from the British Library.

Printed and bound in Singapore

Who Will Sing My Puff-a-bye?

Charlotte Hudson &
Mary McQuillan

To Elena

Charlotte Hudson

THE BODLEY HEAD

LONDON

Crossfire was feeling all out of spark.
Mummy had just got a job as a firelighter in
some unheated volcanoes nearby and now he
didn't know who would look after him.

"Who will tickle my tail in the morning?"
he asked Mummy. "Or cook me
lava pancakes for breakfast?
Who will play I Fry with me
on the way to school?"

"And what about my puff-a-bye? Nobody knows how to sing me to sleep except you."

Crossfire's small snout began to snuffle.

"I'll always be there to sing your puff-a-bye," said Mummy and gave him a huge dragon hug. "But for the next few months I've found someone to help look after you and Puffing Billy."

It was then that
Mummy introduced

Smokescreen.

Smokescreen breathed green smoke.
Smokescreen came from a different country.
Smokescreen spoke in a strange way.

Smokescreen
wasn't Mummy!

The next morning, it was Smokescreen
who woke Crossfire up for school, but she
didn't tickle his tail like Mummy did.

It was Smokescreen who cooked
their lava pancakes, but they weren't
burnt and crispy like Mummy's.

It was Smokescreen who walked them to school,
but she didn't know the rules for I Fry.

And when the school day finished and the
little dragons were let out, it was Smokescreen
who was there to meet him and not Mummy.

"Please don't go to work tomorrow," Crossfire asked Mummy when she came to sing his puff-a-bye that evening. Mummy tickled Crossfire's tail just as she usually did. "Things will be better tomorrow," she said.

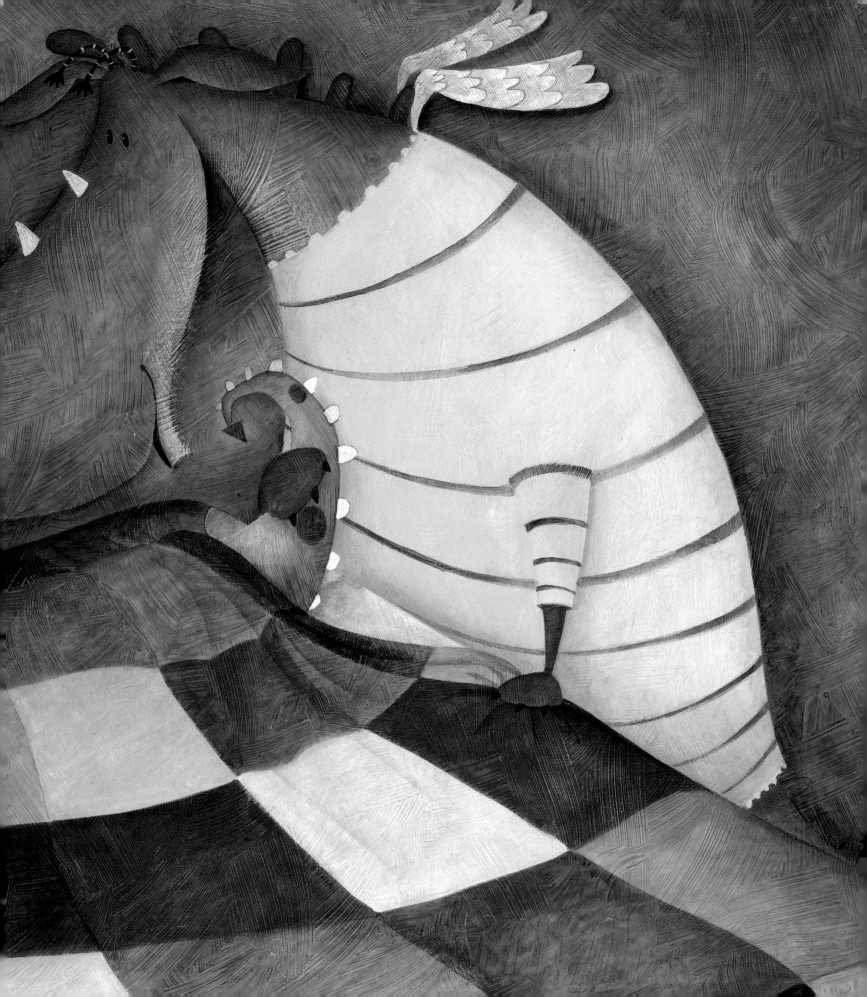

The next morning, Smokescreen cooked
fireballs for breakfast. Crossfire and
Puffing Billy couldn't believe it!

"This is what I eat for breakfast at
home," Smokescreen explained. And even though
of course they couldn't be as good as Mummy's
lava pancakes, they were rather nice.

On the way to school,
they played Down
with St George.

And even though it couldn't
be as good as Mummy's
I Fry, it was rather fun.

At the end of the school day,
Smokescreen was there to meet
Crossfire again. But this time, she put
on a firework display with dragonwheels
and snoutfizzers. Then all the
little dragons wanted to
walk home with her too.

That evening, when Mummy came up to
sing Crossfire his puff-a-bye, he had so much
to talk about that he forgot to ask her not
to go to work the next day.

Fire season came and went, but Crossfire was having so much fun he hardly noticed. Before he knew it, it was time for Smokescreen to go home.

"But who will cook me fireballs in the morning?" he asked Mummy. "Or play Down with St George on the way to school? And who will make dragonwheels and snoutfizzers at the end of the day?" Crossfire's small snout began to snuffle.

Mummy tickled Crossfire's tail. "I know you'll miss Smokescreen," she said. "But for the next few months I've found someone else to help look after you and Puffing Billy."

And then Mummy introduced Bonfire.

Crossfire held his puff and eyed her up and down. "Can you make fireballs for breakfast?" he asked her firmly.

"No," said Bonfire in a small voice.

"Or play Down with St George?" said Crossfire.

"No," said Bonfire in an even smaller voice.

"And what about dragonwheels and snoutfizzers?" Crossfire snorted.

"I don't know about them,"
said Bonfire.

"But I can give rides on my tail!"

And suddenly Crossfire knew that
everything would be all right!